The Art Riddle Contest

Written by Angela Shelf Medearis
Illustrated by Judith DuFour Love

STECK-VAUGHN
ELEMENTARY · SECONDARY · ADULT · LIBRARY

A Harcourt Classroom Education Company

www.steck-vaughn.com

Contents

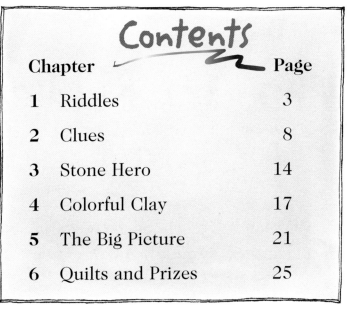

Chapter 1
Riddles

"Class," said Mrs. Lee, "before we leave on our field trip to the art museum, I have a surprise for you."

Stacy Morgan started to smile. She loved surprises. The whole class seemed to be holding their breath. Everyone, that is, except Inky Nelson. Inky's face never changed expression as he listened to Mrs. Lee.

"We're going to have a riddle contest while we're at the museum," Mrs. Lee said. "The winning team will get these art sets."

Mrs. Lee held up the prizes so that everyone could see them. The art sets had packages of colorful molding clay, glitter pens, colored pencils, oil paints, watercolors, acrylic paints, canvases, paintbrushes, a rainbow of colorful fabrics, and construction paper. Stacy had wanted a set like that for as long as she could remember.

"Wow!" said Lucy. "Look at all those pretty colors."

"It even has watercolors and different sized paintbrushes," Stacy said.

"These paints and brushes are similar to the ones the artists used to create the works you'll see at the art museum," Mrs. Lee said.

Wow!

"Now, let me clue you in to what you'll see at the museum," Mrs. Lee said. "Remember, art is an expression of the thoughts, experiences, and feelings of the artists. They use different types of materials to create their work. You'll see art made from stone, fabric, and clay. You'll see paintings that have been stroked, splashed, dribbled, and sprayed onto a canvas."

"Some art you'll see could cover a bed or a wall. Other art will show a man made out of stone or paintings of people holding clay objects. Some art will even show you a big picture of history."

cool!

PEN PALS

CLAY

5

Mrs. Lee handed out the riddles to the class. "You'll each work with a partner. You'll need to discuss these riddles, work together to solve them, and write down your answers," Mrs. Lee said.

? ? ? Riddles ? ? ?

1. My last name is made of two words put together. One word names an object and the other word names the material that it is often made of. I also write and illustrate books for children. Who am I?

_____

2. I am a woman. I used a chisel and hammer to make my art. Who am I?

_____

3. I cover a big area when I paint. Most artists hang their art on a wall. I prefer to paint right on the wall. Who am I?

_____

4. My art shows people from my culture. It can be found in a part of this museum that tells where I live. Who am I?

_____

"Now please line up when I call your name," said Mrs. Lee. "Nicky Sanders and Lucy Miller. Stacy Morgan and Inky Nelson, you two will be partners for the trip," she said with a smile.

Nicky Sanders laughed when he heard Inky's name and whispered something to Lucy, his partner. Stacy frowned at him.

Inky didn't seem to notice. He was writing in his notebook.

Stacy looked at Inky. He rarely said anything. In order to solve the riddles, they'd have to talk to each other to figure out the answers. How could she get Inky Nelson interested in solving the riddles?

Chapter 2
Clues

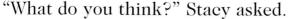

Stacy and Inky sat side by side on the ride to the museum. Inky never looked up from his notebook. Suddenly Stacy had an idea.

"May I borrow a sheet of paper from you?" Stacy asked Inky. "I feel like drawing."

Inky didn't say anything. He just tore a sheet out of his notebook and handed it to Stacy.

Stacy thought for a moment. Then she drew a picture of a ballerina. She showed it to Inky.

"What do you think?" Stacy asked.

Inky looked at the drawing for a long time. Then he smiled at Stacy.

"Not bad," Inky said, "it's not bad at all. I like to draw, too."

Inky opened his notebook and showed it to Stacy. It was filled with page after page of ink drawings.

"Wow! You are good," Stacy said.

"Thanks," Inky said.

"I didn't know you could draw like this," Stacy said.

"What does Inky Nelson have inside that notebook?" Nicky asked. "May I see it?"

"It's no big deal," Inky said. "It's just a bunch of doodles and sketches that I've done. I guess you can see it."

"Ooh!" said Lucy as she looked at Inky's notebook.

"Cool!" said Nicky. "I thought your notebook would be filled with spelling words and math problems." He passed the notebook back over the seat to Inky.

Stacy took the notebook and looked at it again. "Inky, I think you're an ARTIST!" she said.

"I love art," Inky said. "Pen and ink drawings are my favorite. I also like to draw with charcoal pencils."

"Me, too," said Stacy. "But I especially like watercolors! That's why I want to win the riddle contest. I would love to have one of those art sets. Those sets are awesome!"

"So would I," said Inky. "Maybe we'll win. I wrote down the clues Mrs. Lee gave us."

"What clues?" Stacy asked.

"Don't you remember when Mrs. Lee said *clue* when she talked about the museum? She said that some of the art could cover a wall or a bed, show a man made of stone, or show people holding clay objects. And she also said that the art could show a big picture of history," Inky said. "I think she was giving us four clues to help us answer the riddles."

"You're right!" Stacy said. "I'll bet you're the only one who wrote down those clues!"

CLUES

1. art that can cover a wall or bed

2. a man made of stone

3. people holding clay objects

4. a big picture of history

"I write everything down. Or I draw a picture of it so that I can remember," Inky said.

"So," Stacy said, "that is why everyone calls you Inky!"

"I guess," Inky said. "I never go anywhere without my ink pens."

Suddenly, Mrs. Lee said, "Here we are, class."

The art museum was a beautiful building surrounded by marble statues.

"I know this museum like the back of my hand," Inky said. "I've even got a list of all my favorite works of art."

"You do? You must come here all the time," Stacy said.

"I come here just about every weekend," Inky said. "My mom works here as a guide on Saturdays. This is one of my favorite places! The artists here used everything from recycled trash to solid gold paint to make their works. There's some amazing art here. Wait until you see it!"

Chapter 3
Stone Hero

"Class, this museum has many pieces of art. Some art pieces are very large and others are small. We are about to walk by a large piece of art now. Let's stop and take a closer look," said Mrs. Lee.

Everyone looked at the stone sculptures. "Look at all the detail the artist used," Mrs. Lee said. "Doesn't this statue look realistic?"

Stacy pointed to the cold, hard stone. "This must have taken a long time to make," Stacy whispered to Inky.

"It did," Inky said. "My mom said the sculptor first made it out of plaster. Then she used a chisel and a hammer to carve it in stone. It took over a year to finish."

"She?" asked Stacy. "You mean a woman carved this statue?"

"Yes," Inky said. "The sculptor's name is Elisabet Ney. That's a sculpture of a Texas hero."

"A man made of stone," Stacy said. "Wasn't that one of the clues you wrote down?"

"Yes," said Inky. "That is one of the clues."

"So Elisabet Ney is the answer to one of the riddles!" said Stacy.

"Let's see," said Inky. "One of our riddles was about a woman who used a chisel and a hammer to make art. I'd say it's Elisabet Ney."

"Then we've got our first answer. Hurry and write it down," said Stacy excitedly.

Inky wrote the answer beside number two.

1.

2. Elisabet Ney

3.

The first floor inside the art museum had sculptures and wall after wall of brightly colored paintings. Some artists used watercolors and oils. Others used pieces of fabric or torn paper. Stacy had never seen so many beautiful works of art.

"Stay with your partner and meet me back here in an hour," Mrs. Lee said.

"Everyone else will probably start down here. I think we should start on the third floor," Inky said. "We'll see things better if no one else is around."

"Great idea," Stacy said. "I can't wait to see all the art."

"I can't wait to see the art and to solve the other riddles," Inky said.

Chapter 4
Colorful Clay

"This is the Southwest Gallery," Inky said. "Most of the art here was created by artists in Texas and New Mexico."

Inky looked carefully at all the paintings. "Oh, look at this one," he said. "It's by Georgia O'Keeffe. It looks like the light glows right through it."

"It does," Stacy said. "I would have never noticed that. How do you think she did that?"

"I guess it's the colors and the objects she chose," Inky said. "I think it's also the way she put the paint on the canvas. You can't even see any brushstrokes. My mom calls it the artist's technique. She says that each artist works differently, even if they're using the same kind of paint."

"Look at these big blocks of colors," Stacy said as they wandered into another room.

"That artist's name is Amado Peña. He uses acrylic paints when he works," Inky said. "That's what makes his paintings so colorful."

"Look at the designs on the clay pots in the painting," said Stacy.

"Clay pots! That sounds like one of the clues," said Inky.

"So do you think Amado Peña is an answer to one of the riddles?" asked Stacy. Inky and Stacy looked at their riddle sheets. "Look at number four," said Stacy.

Inky read the riddle and said, "Stacy, you're right! Amado Peña is the answer. Peña lives in Texas and New Mexico. That's the Southwest part of the United States. And his paintings do show people from his culture." Inky wrote Peña's name by number four.

"Now, we're two clues closer to winning the art sets," said Stacy.

"We only have two riddles left—let's get going," Inky said. "Let's go downstairs and look at the rest of the museum."

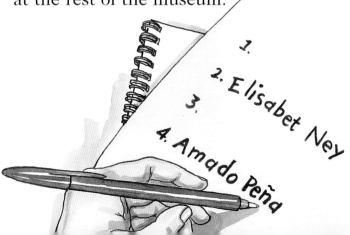

1.
2. Elisabet Ney
3.
4. Amado Peña

Chapter 5
The Big Picture

"This is where all the murals are displayed," Inky said.

"What's a mural?" asked Stacy.

"Murals are pieces of art painted right on a wall or a ceiling," said Inky. "They're so big that it's easier to see the details if you stand in the middle of the room."

Stacy looked around. The room was filled with paintings that started near the ceiling and went down to the floor. They were HUGE!

"These murals are like the works of Diego Rivera," Inky said. "We studied about him in art class, remember?"

"Oh, yes," Stacy said. "As a matter of fact, it says here that this artist was taught by Rivera. His name is Hale Woodruff," she said reading the display sign. "This mural shows the settling of African Americans in California."

Inky studied the mural more closely. "This mural takes up the entire wall. It's massive!" he said.

Stacy and Inky stared upward at the mural. "This is a fun way to learn about history," said Inky.

"This is one BIG picture of history," said Stacy.

"That's it," said Inky. "A big picture of history. That's one of Mrs. Lee's clues."

Inky and Stacy looked at the list of riddles. "This mural certainly covers a big area. So Hale Woodruff has to be the answer to number three," said Stacy.

Inky wrote Woodruff's name by number three.

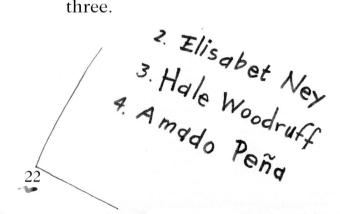

2. Elisabet Ney
3. Hale Woodruff
4. Amado Peña

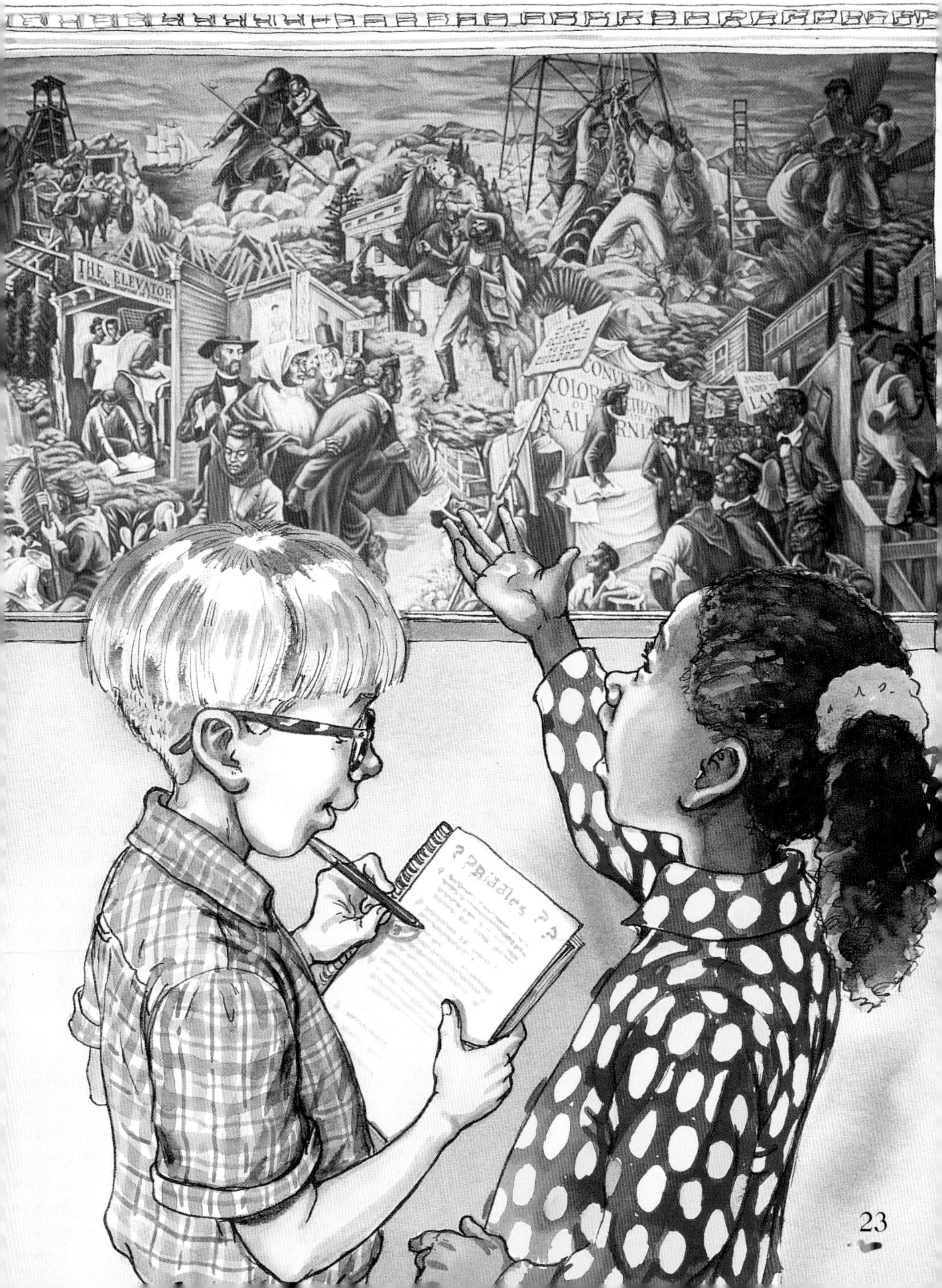
THE ELEVATOR
CONVENTION
Riddles

Stacy said, "Isn't it amazing that Woodruff was able to paint such a large area?"

"It sure is," said Inky. "Murals are just awesome!"

"I've always wanted to paint a mural," said Stacy.

"Me, too," replied Inky.

Inky looked down at his list of clues and thought for a minute. Then he said, "We've just got to win those art sets. The last clue says that the art can cover a bed or a wall. Hmmm. I bet that art is made of cloth or something. Art like that is down on the first floor. Come on, let's go!"

Stacy and Inky hurried down the stairs.

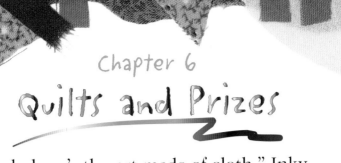

Chapter 6
Quilts and Prizes

"Look, here's the art made of cloth," Inky said. "Now we just need to use the last clue to solve riddle number one."

Stacy and Inky looked at the different pieces of art made from cloth. Each one was unique and interesting. Then Inky and Stacy stood in front of a beautiful quilt. Inky said, "I think I've got the answer to our clue."

"What is it?" asked Stacy. Inky pointed at the quilt. "A quilt?" asked Stacy.

"That's right. It will cover a bed or a wall. Won't it?" asked Inky.

"Okay," said Stacy. "Now let's find the answer to the riddle."

Stacy and Inky stared at the quilt. "Look, the artist has written a story in the border. It's called *Tar Beach*," said Stacy.

"*Tar Beach,*" said Inky. "That is one of my sister's favorite books. I think it is written by Faith Ringgold."

"So this art is a quilt and a story," said Stacy.

"Hey, wait a minute. *Ring* and *gold*!" Inky said. "The artist's last name is two words put together. They name an object and the material that it is often made of. That's part of riddle number one."

"And she also writes children's books," said Stacy. "We've done it! We've solved all the riddles. Let's go find Mrs. Lee!"

Inky and Stacy walked through the museum as fast as they could. Finally they spotted Mrs. Lee, but…

1. Faith Ringgold

2. Elisabet Ney

A group of students were already gathered around Mrs. Lee. It looked like Lucy and Nicky were reading their answers to the riddles.

"Oh, no!" Stacy said. "They're going to win the contest and the art sets."

"Let's go see," Inky said. "Maybe we still have a chance."

Just as Inky and Stacy joined the others, Mrs. Lee said, "I'm sorry, Nicky and Lucy. You have three of the riddles right, but you missed the first one. Keep looking for the answer. It's right here on this floor."

Nicky and Lucy walked away looking disappointed.

Mrs. Lee asked, "Did any other partners solve all the riddles?"

"We did! We did!" Stacy said. "Go ahead and read our answers, Inky."

"Me?" Inky asked Stacy. "Really?"

"Come on, you can do it," Stacy said.

Inky looked at Stacy. Then he looked around at the class. Everyone was staring at him. He cleared his throat. He opened his mouth, but no sound came out.

"Go ahead," Stacy whispered to him. "You know the answers."

Inky coughed. Then he slowly read each answer.

Mrs. Lee smiled. "Class," she said. "We have our winners. Inky and Stacy have answered all the questions correctly."

Stacy and Inky smiled as they took their seat next to each other on the bus. "We did it! We won the contest," Inky said excitedly to Stacy.

"You sure know your art," said Stacy.

"So do you," said Inky. "I can't wait to use the acrylic paints in the art set to paint bright colors like Amado Peña."

"Maybe you can use the paints to create a giant mural," Stacy said.

Inky said, "We could paint one together! Who knows, maybe someday people will be looking at our art on the walls of a museum."

"That would be so cool," Stacy said. "Do you think we can get started on that mural right away?"

"We'll need a wall," Inky said. "Do you know of one we can use?"

"Not at home. Maybe Mrs. Lee could talk to the principal about letting us paint a mural on a wall at school," Stacy said.

"Or she may let us use a piece of fabric like Faith Ringgold did and hang it up," Inky said.

"That's a wonderful idea," said Stacy. "I can't wait to ask. We could paint a mural or a quilt about all the artists we saw at the museum."

"Then we could invite other classes to come and see it," Inky said. "It would be like a museum right in our own school."

"Let's ask her right away when we get back," said Stacy.

"You know, we make a great team!" said Inky.
"You mean great ARTISTS," laughed Stacy.